The Palm Tree Swingers Island Band

Lily Lawson

Published by

THE
WRIGHT HOUSE

The tiger played harmonica.

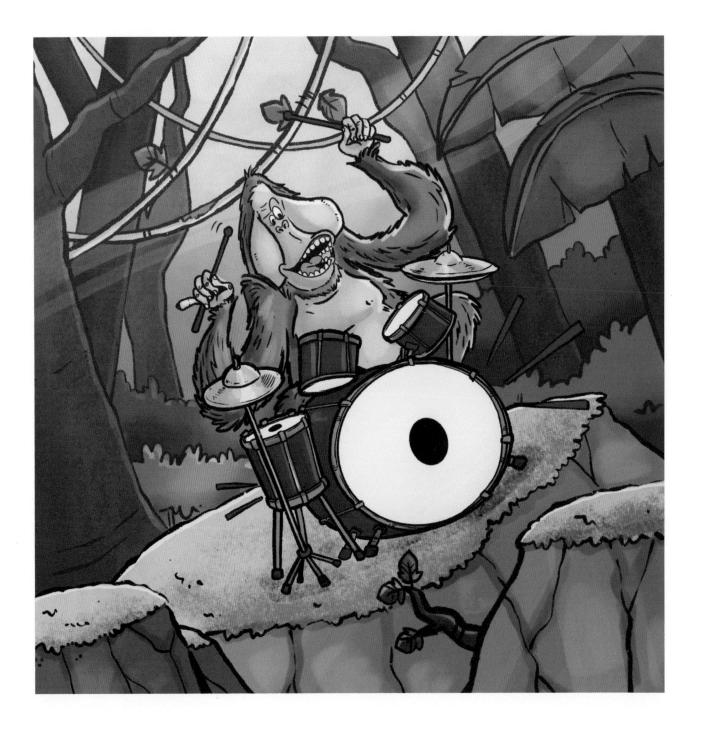

The orangutan banged the drums.

With the elephant on piano, this was no time for the glums.

The eagle sang soprano.

The rhino took the bass.

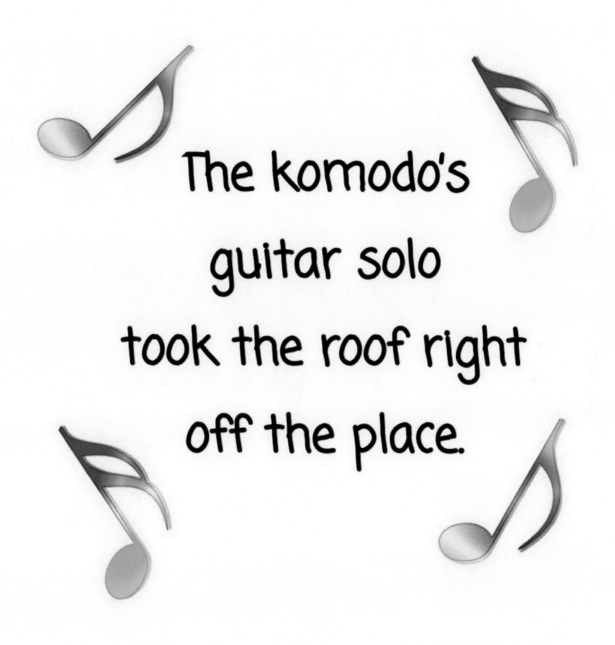

The komodo's guitar solo took the roof right off the place.

The spider was a
harpist.

The turtle rocked trombone.

You didn't have
to be there
you could hear it
all at home.

They really
were quite famous,
The Palm Tree
Swingers
Island Band.

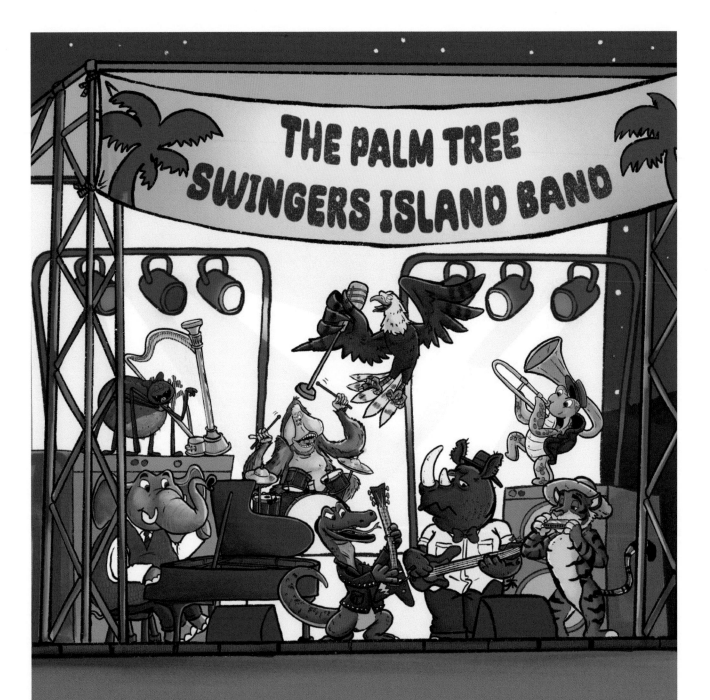

By the author

Santa's Early Christmas

Last year Santa was hungry and thirsty by the time he delivered all the presents.
But when he came home there was no food and drink left!
This year Santa decides things are going to be different.

Palm Tree Swinger's Island Band

Take a tiger, an orangutan, an elephant, an eagle,
a rhino, a dragon, a spider, and a turtle.
Mix with music till loud – you might want to stand back.

If I Were Invisible

Think of all the things we could get away with if nobody could see us!
But how long would the fun last if we had to do it all alone?

Acknowledgements

Thank so much to my illustrator Gustyawan.

To Louise for the prompt that inspired
the original version of this poem.

To Cheryl for her patience with me.

To Ann for the Indonesian conversations.

All errors are entirely mine.

To Dreena, Jo, Becky, Elise, Alex, and all at WWs.

To Anita, Kim, and Cin.

To Team Tea and Books.

To Butterfly who inspires me every day.

To Christine.

To my dad.

And to all of you for reading my book.

About the author

Lily Lawson is a poet and fiction writer living in the UK.
She has poetry, short stories, and creative non-fiction
published in anthologies and online in addition to her poetry books

My Fathers Daughter,
A Taste of What's to Come,
and Rainbow's Red Book of Poetry

and her kids' books
Santa's Early Christmas,
The Palm Tree Swingers Island Band
and If I Were Invisible…

You can find out more about Lily and read more of her work on her blog.

Subscribers to Life with Lily are the first to hear all her writing news.
You can sign up here.

Printed in Great Britain
by Amazon

22524741R00021